Ladybird Readers

# Sideswipe Loses His Head

## Series Editor: Sorrel Pitts
## Adapted by Anne Collins

LADYBIRD BOOKS

UK | USA | Canada | Ireland | Australia
India | New Zealand | South Africa

Ladybird Books is part of the Penguin Random House group of companies
whose addresses can be found at global.penguinrandomhouse.com.
www.penguin.co.uk    www.puffin.co.uk    www.ladybird.co.uk

Penguin
Random House
UK

First published 2017
001

Licensed by:

Printed in China

A CIP catalogue record for this book is available from the British Library

ISBN: 978–0–241–29889–3

All correspondence to
Ladybird Books
Penguin Random House Children's
80 Strand, London WC2R 0RL

MIX
Paper from
responsible sources
FSC® C018179

# Sideswipe Loses His Head

# Picture words

## Autobots

Bumblebee

Sideswipe

Strongarm

Grimlock

Fixit

# Vertebreak
(a Decepticon)

tunnel

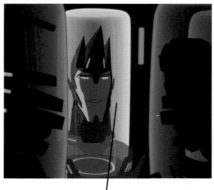

jar

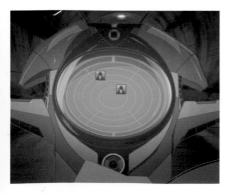

scanner

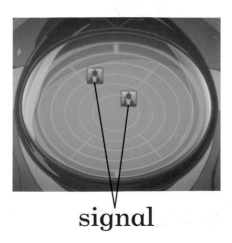

signal

One day, the Autobots heard that a Decepticon called Vertebreak was in a train tunnel near them.

They went to find him as fast as they could, because they wanted to stop him from doing something bad.

Sideswipe was very fast, so he arrived at the tunnel first. He called Bumblebee and Strongarm.

"I'm here!" he said. "I'm faster than all of you!"

"Stay in the tunnel and wait for us, Sideswipe," said Bumblebee.

"I will," said Sideswipe.

Suddenly, Sideswipe heard a noise. He turned around, but it was too late.

Vertebreak came out of the tunnel and hit Sideswipe! Sideswipe shouted and fell down.

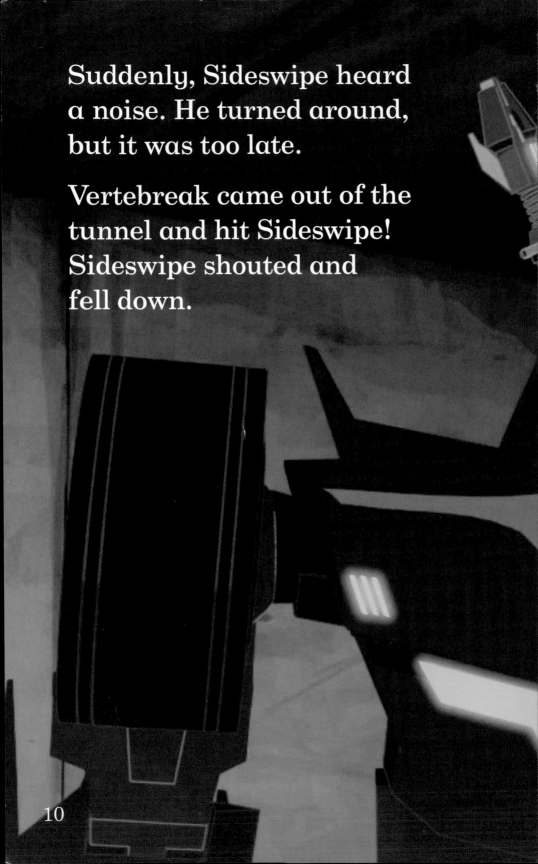

When Sideswipe woke up, he was lying on a table in a strange room, and he couldn't move. Then, he saw Vertebreak.

"Who are you?" asked Sideswipe.

"No one important," said Vertebreak. "Not like you. You're a wonderful robot—fast and strong."

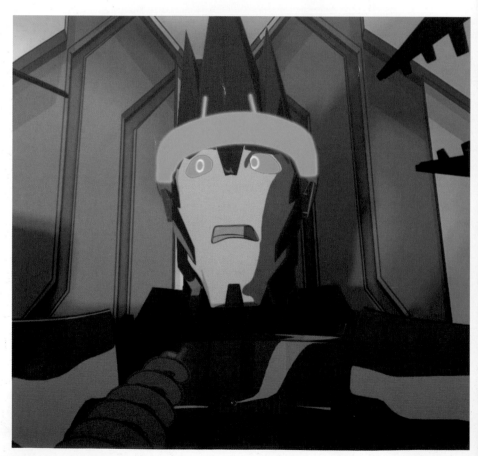

Then, Vertebreak started to laugh.

"This isn't funny!" said Sideswipe.

The Autobots were looking for Sideswipe in the tunnel.

Fixit was looking at his scanner. He was worried. "There's a problem," he said. "I'm getting TWO signals for Sideswipe."

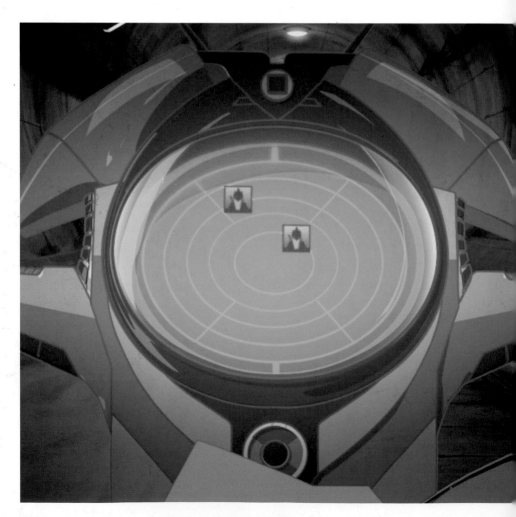

He pointed to a tunnel. "The stronger signal is coming from there," he said.

So Bumblebee and Fixit walked into the tunnel.

A moment later, Bumblebee saw a robot far down the dark tunnel.

"Sideswipe!" he called. "Is that you?"

The robot looked like Sideswipe, but it picked up something heavy and threw it at Bumblebee!

"Fixit!" shouted Bumblebee. "Is that Sideswipe or not?"

"Yes," answered Fixit. "And . . . no."

When the strange robot moved into the light, Bumblebee and Fixit were very surprised. The robot had Sideswipe's body, but Vertebreak's head!

"Where's Sideswipe?" asked Bumblebee.

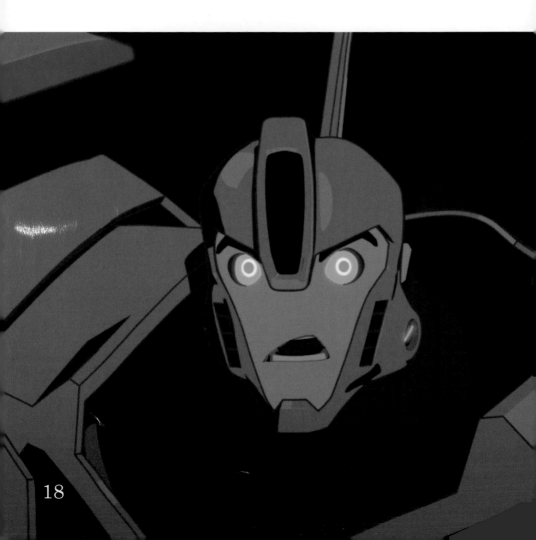

"He's here," said Vertebreak,
and he laughed. "Well . . . most
of him is here!"

"Sideswipe's body is MY body now!" said Vertebreak.

"Where's Sideswipe?" asked Bumblebee, again.

"He's fine," said Vertebreak.

Bumblebee ran and tried to hit Vertebreak, but Vertebreak threw him to the ground.

A train came past, and Vertebreak
hid behind it.

"Fixit, do you still have the other signal on your scanner?" asked Bumblebee.

"Yes," said Fixit, "but it hasn't moved."

"Good," said Bumblebee. "Let's follow the signal."

Fixit stopped at a broken part of the wall. "Sideswipe must be in there," he said.

Bumblebee pushed the wall, and a door opened to show a tunnel behind it.

Now, Bumblebee and Fixit were in a strange room. They could hear Sideswipe calling.

They turned around, but they couldn't see him.

"Where are you, Sideswipe?" shouted Bumblebee.

"I'm over here!" called Sideswipe.

Bumblebee turned around and saw a glass jar at the back of a shelf. Sideswipe's head was inside the jar!

"Are you all right?" said Bumblebee.

"I've had better days!" said Sideswipe. "Repair me!"

"We need to quickly find your body," Fixit said, "or we won't be able to save you."

Back in the tunnel, Strongarm and Grimlock were fighting Vertebreak.

First, Vertebreak kicked Grimlock, then he kicked Strongarm, hard.

Strongarm fell to the ground. Grimlock ran quickly to help her, but a train came into the tunnel and hit him!

Strongarm called Bumblebee for help

Bumblebee picked up the jar with Sideswipe's head.

"I can't help Strongarm and Grimlock to fight Vertebreak," Sideswipe said sadly. "I'm no good without my body."

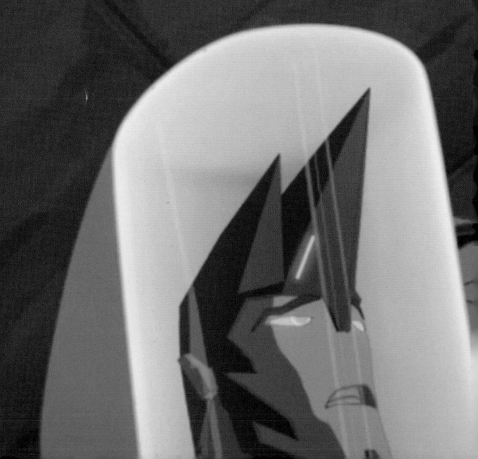

"Don't say that," said Bumblebee. "You're a fast robot, but that's not all. You're also an important part of our group."

Bumblebee found Strongarm in the tunnel. When she saw the jar with Sideswipe's head, Strongarm was very surprised.

"Where's Grimlock?" asked Bumblebee.

The next moment, they heard a noise.

"Follow me!" said Bumblebee.
Strongarm picked up the jar and
ran after Bumblebee.

Grimlock was fighting Vertebreak! Bumblebee and Strongarm ran to help him.

Sideswipe felt sad because he couldn't help the Autobots.

Then, he had an idea.

"I CAN help you," he called.
"He's using MY body, so I know
what he's going to do!"

Sideswipe told the Autobots how to fight Vertebreak.

"Hit him, Bumblebee!" he shouted. "Move away, Strongarm! Now, kick him, Grimlock!"

The Autobots did what Sideswipe told them, and soon Vertebreak fell down.

He lay on the ground with his eyes closed.

"Good work, everyone!"
said Bumblebee.

"And I helped you all to win!"
said Sideswipe happily.

Fixit repaired Sideswipe, and put his head back on his body.

"You're all right now, Sideswipe," he said, "but I need to make sure I repaired everything correctly. So don't move too fast for now!"

"No problem," said Sideswipe. "I've learned that I'm a fast robot, but that's not all. I'm good at other things, too!"

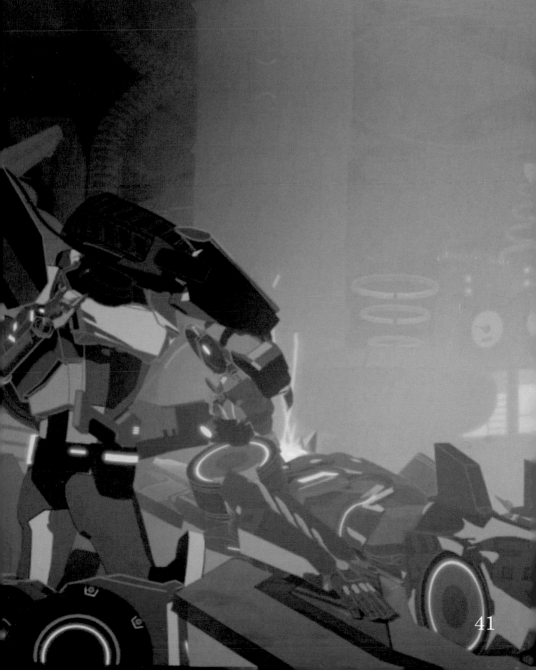

Then, Sideswipe said, "But . . . I AM still the fastest robot of us all!"

"Really?" said Strongarm. "Let's have a race home."

Strongarm drove away quickly, and Bumblebee and Grimlock followed her.

Sideswipe tried to catch them, but he couldn't move fast enough.

"Don't worry, Sideswipe!" said Fixit. "You'll be the fastest robot again soon."

# Activities

The key below describes the skills practiced in each activity.

🖊 Spelling and writing

📖 Reading

💬 Speaking

❓ Critical thinking

✳ Preparation for the Cambridge Young Learners Exams

**1** **Find the words and write them on the lines.** 📖 ✏️

orjarbltbfeslppehosbtunnelabwlsignalopheaddjhuojitrainjiscannert

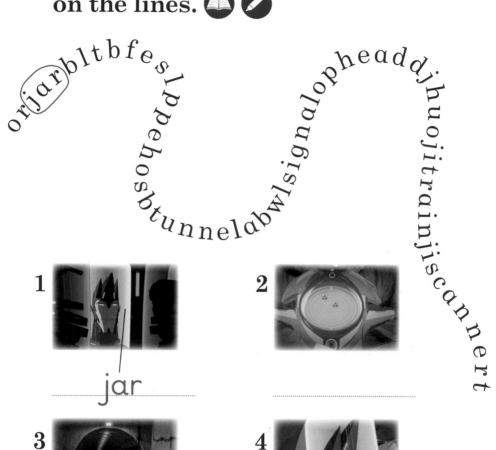

**1**

jar

**2**

**3**

**4**

**5**

**6**

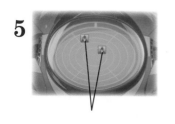

**2** **Look and read. Choose the correct words and write them on the lines.**

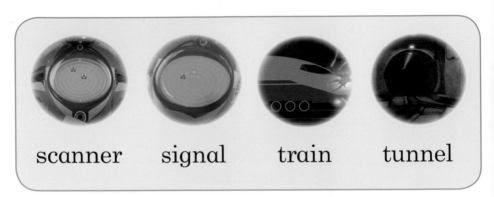

scanner    signal    train    tunnel

**1** Fixit was looking at his ___scanner___.

**2** Bumblebee saw a robot far down the dark _____.

**3** A _____ came past, and Vertebreak hid behind it.

**4** "Fixit, do you still have the other _____ on your scanner?" asked Bumblebee.

**Write the missing letters.**

esw   iml   ixi   ebr   ong

**1**   Sid e s w ipe

**2**   Gr _____ ock

**3** 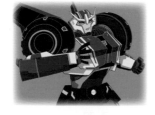  Str _____ arm

**4**   F _____ t

**5**   Vert _____ eak

**4** Put a ✓ by the names of the Transformers in this story. 📖 ❓

1 Bumblebee ✓    2 Ratchet ☐

3 Cliffjumper ☐    4 Scanner ☐

5 Fixit ☐    6 Sideswipe ☐

7 Grimlock ☐    8 Strongarm ☐

9 Vertebreak ☐    10 Signal ☐

**5** **Read the text. Choose the correct words and write them on the lines.**

| 1 | A | An | One |
| 2 | in | on | under |
| 3 | as fast as | faster than | fastest |
| 4 | someone | something | somewhere |

[1] _____One_____ day, the Autobots

heard that a Decepticon called Vertebreak

was [2] _____ a train tunnel

near them. They went to find him

[3] _____ they could,

because they wanted to stop him from

doing [4] _____ bad.

## 6 Read and write *Although* or *so*.

**1**  Sideswipe was very fast, ......so...... he arrived at the tunnel first.

**2**  ........................ Sideswipe turned around, it was too late.

**3**  Vertebreak hit Sideswipe, ........................ he fell down.

**4**  ........................ he woke up, Sideswipe couldn't move.

**7** Look and read. Put a ✓ by the
correct pictures.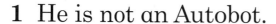

**1** He is not an Autobot.

a

b ✓

**2** He can repair things.

a

b

**3** Sideswipe's head is in this.

a

b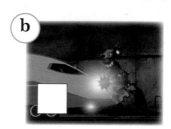

**4** This can find signals.

a

b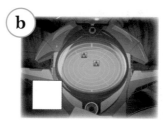

**8** **Circle the correct answers.**

**1** "Stay in the tunnel and wait for us, Sideswipe," said Bumblebee.

  **a** "I can," said Sideswipe.

  **b** "I will," said Sideswipe.

**2** "Who are you?" asked Sideswipe.

  **a** "No one important," said Vertebreak.

  **b** "Nothing important," said Vertebreak.

**3** "Where's Sideswipe?" asked Bumblebee, again.

  **a** "He's fine," said Vertebreak.

  **b** "I'm fine," said Vertebreak.

**4** "Are you all right?" said Bumblebee.

  **a** "It's okay!" said Sideswipe.

  **b** "I've had better days!" said Sideswipe.

## 9  Read and write the correct form of the verbs. 📖 ✏️

1
Sideswipe ___called___ **(call)** Bumblebee and Strongarm.

2
When Sideswipe woke up, he _____ **(lie)** on a table in a strange room.

3
The Autobots _____ **(look)** for Sideswipe in the tunnel.

4
Fixit _____ **(look)** at his scanner.

5
"The stronger signal _____ **(come)** from there," said Fixit.

**10** **Look and read. Write the correct words on the lines.** 📖 ✏️

**1**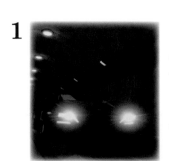
Sideswipe was very fast, so he arrived at the tunnel ~~last~~.

_first_

**2**
"This ~~is~~ funny!" said Sideswipe.

**3**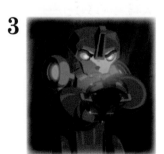
Fixit was ~~happy~~. "There's a problem," he said.

**4**
Bumblebee saw a robot far down the ~~light~~ tunnel.

**11** **Look at the letters.**
**Write the words.** 📖 ✏️ ✦

1 ( n e t l u n )

Sideswipe was very fast so he
arrived at the ____tunnel____ first.

2 ( b o t o r )

"You're a wonderful _____
—fast and strong."

3 ( n a l s i g s )

"There's a problem," Fixit said.
"I'm getting TWO _____
for Sideswipe."

4 ( n a s c e r n )

"Fixit, do you still have the other
signal on your _____?"
asked Bumblebee.

## 12 Look and read. Circle the correct words. 📖

**1**  Sideswipe turned around, but it was too (late.) / lately.

**2**  Sideswipe was lying on a table in a **strange** / **strangely** room.

**3**  The robot picked up something **heavy.** / **heavily.**

**4**  "We need to **quick** / **quickly** find your body." Fixit said.

**13** Work with a friend. Talk about the two pictures. How are they different? 💬

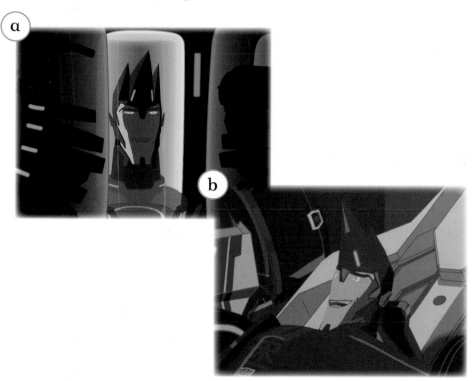

a

b

In picture a, Sideswipe's head is not on his body.

In picture b, Sideswipe's head is on his body.

**14** **Complete the sentences.**
**Write a—d.** 📖

**1** Bumblebee ran and tried to
hit Vertebreak,                                        d

**2** A train came past,                        .....................

**3** Bumblebee pushed the wall,        .....................

**4** Bumblebee and Fixit could
hear Sideswipe calling,                    .....................

**a** and Vertebreak hid behind it.

**b** and a door opened to show
a tunnel behind it.

**c** but they couldn't see him.

**d** but Vertebreak
threw him to
the ground.

**15** Work with a friend. Ask and answer questions about the Transformers. 🗨️ ❓

**1** *Which Transformer do you like the best?*

*I like Bumblebee the best.*

**2** Why do you like him / her?
What can he / she do?

**3** Who is not nice in the story?

**4** Why don't you like him / her?

## 16 Write *still* or *yet*.

**1**

"Fixit, do you ___**still**___ have the other signal on your scanner?"

**2**

"Yes," said Fixit, "but it hasn't moved _____."

**3**

They could hear Sideswipe, but they _____ couldn't see him.

**4**

"You're all right now, Sideswipe, but don't move too fast _____."

**5**

"I AM _____ the fastest robot of us all," said Sideswipe.

**17** **Write the names of the robots on the correct lines.** ✏️ ❓

Bumblebee

Grimlock

Sideswipe

Fixit

Vertebreak

Which robot . . .

**1** is strong and a good fighter, but very heavy?  Grimlock

**2** is bad, but very clever?

**3** repairs things and follows signals?

**4** is very fast?

**5** is black and yellow?

**18** **Write the questions. Then write the answers.** 📖 ✏️

**1** ( Was ) ( Vertebreak ) ( Autobot ) ( an ) ( ? )

Question: _Was Vertebreak an Autobot?_

Answer: _No, he wasn't._

**2** ( looking ) ( Fixit ) ( at ) ( Was ) ( scanner ) ( his ) ( ? )

Question: ........................................................

........................................................

Answer: ........................................................

**3** ( all ) ( Sideswipe ) ( right ) ( Was ) ( ? )

Question: ........................................................

........................................................

Answer: ........................................................

**19** Talk to a friend about the story.
Answer the questions. 🗨 ✪

**1** What's happening in this picture?

Grimlock and Vertebreak are fighting.

**2** What has happened to Sideswipe?

**3** How does he help the Autobots?

**4** What happens at the end of the story?

# Level 4

**The Pied Piper of Hamelin**

978–0–241–25378–6 ☐

**The Wizard of Oz**

978–0–241–25379–3 ☐

**Sam and the Robots**

978–0–241–25380–9 ☐

**The Little Mermaid**

978–0–241–29874–9 ☐

**Space**

978–0–241–25381–6 ☐

**Pinocchio**

978–0–241–28430–8 ☐

**Alice in Wonderland**

978–0–241–28431–5 ☐

**Under the Oceans**

978–0–241–29888–6 ☐

**Knights and Castles**

978–0–241–28432–2 ☐

**Heidi**

978–0–241–28433–9 ☐

**Peter and the Wolf**

978–0–241–28434–6 ☐

**Dangerous Journeys**

978-0-241-29891-6 ☐

**A Fight with Underbite**

978-0-241-29890-9 ☐

**Sideswipe Loses his Head**

978-0-241-29889-3 ☐